THE BULL THAT WAS TERRIFICO

THE BULL
THAT WAS
TERRIFICO

by Karel Jaeger

WITH ILLUSTRATIONS BY

CAM

THE JOHN DAY COMPANY
NEW YORK

This book is dedicated with much love to Jane Elizabeth Bangay (Widgy) for a skilled performance of the Backward Ballet, and to Nicholas Stuart Jaeger for a pass to Midhurst.

Signed: THE ODIOUS FROG

THE BULL THAT WAS TERRIFICO

First Capitulo

IN Spain, in the town of El Zapato, in an old Castillo that stood upon a hill, there once lived a famous Spanish Matador called Don Navidad

Lunes Barcelo. He was tall and thin, proud and rich, and almost modest. On his long, sun-baked face he grew smooth, black side-whiskers that curled towards his aristocratic nose. Being a famous Matador, his shiny black hair was shaped to a sort of pigtail and tied with a red bow.

Don Barcelo was married to a beautiful lady called Dona Isabella Verano Primavera Barcelo. They had a son who was fourteen years old. He had been christened Lunes Martes Miercoles Jueves Sabado Domingo Barcelo. As he was a modest boy, he preferred to be known as Zonta.

Zonta expected that one day he too would grow smooth, black side-whiskers like his Papa, but he never expected to become a famous Matador. That was too much to expect.

Every morning Don Barcelo rode out from his old Castillo on a beautiful Caballo. Beside him, on a smaller but still beautiful Caballo, rode Zonta. They both wore large sombreros, white silk shirts, red waistcoats, and wide baggy trousers that were made from fine, black cloth. Their

black riding-boots had long spurs that shone like silver. Dangling from a wrist, the famous Matador carried a long thonged stock-whip which he cracked and swished most skilfully. The Caballos were gaily caparisoned and pranced majestically over the cobbled streets of El Zapato.

"Clippety clop . . . clippety clop . . . clop."

The townsfolk cheered the Matador as he rode away towards the wide and rugged Campo where Señor Martillo, the Bull-grower, grew fierce fighting bulls for the Matador to kill in the arenas of Spain.

"Bravo . . . bravo, Don Barcelo!" cried the people. "May you live to be a hundred."

"*Gracias . . . gracias*," said the Matador, and his large brown eyes rolled round and round in glee.

He liked to be cheered.

"One day, my Zonta, they will cheer you, too."

Zonta smiled thinly because he was modest.

Then, with a great crack of the long whip, father and son spurred their Caballos into a gallop and galloped away across the dusty, sun-baked Campo.

"Clippety clop . . . clop . . . clop . . . clop."

And Dona Isabella Verano Primavera Barcelo waved from the top of the old Castillo.

Second Capitulo

In the old Castillo that stood upon a hill, Don
Barcelo slept in a four-poster bed surrounded by

pictures of bulls he had fought in the arenas. He felt very sorry for the bulls he had killed — so he became a vegetarian.

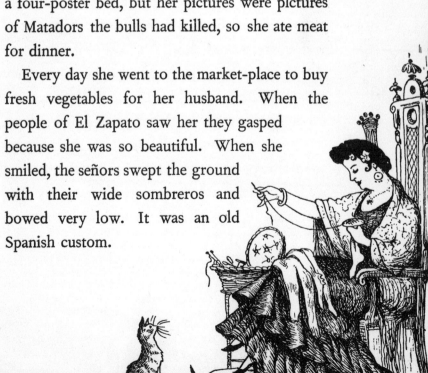

Zonta slept in a smaller four-poster bed surrounded by pictures of bulls he hoped he would never have to fight. They all looked so fierce. Sometimes Zonta thought they looked TOO fierce, so he hid under the bed-clothes.

The beautiful Dona Barcelo spent much of her time weaving and darning socks. She also slept in a four-poster bed, but her pictures were pictures of Matadors the bulls had killed, so she ate meat for dinner.

Every day she went to the market-place to buy fresh vegetables for her husband. When the people of El Zapato saw her they gasped because she was so beautiful. When she smiled, the señors swept the ground with their wide sombreros and bowed very low. It was an old Spanish custom.

Third Capitulo

EVERYONE was contented in El Zapato. The warm sun shone from a clear blue sky. The men rose early and then slept all day in the shade of Naranja trees. They were lazy and fat, but very contented. When the cool evening came they yawned and then strolled down the cobbled streets to drink red wine at the Paradiso Café. There they talked of bulls and matadors and Naranjas and listened to gay music played on Spanish guitars.

The women worked all day, and their houses were always clean and tidy, with whitewashed walls and dark oak beams and exquisitely tiled fireplaces. Large jars of oil and wine stood in cool corners. Spanish onions hung from the rafters and large copper pots hung from nails around the fireplace.

At the end of the main cobbled street there was a little white house surrounded by Naranja trees. It had a balcony decorated with pink geraniums. Here, Señorita Estrella, the most beautiful girl in El Zapato, lived with her father, Señor Pardo. He was a poor schoolmaster. Estrella was fourteen years old. Ever since the time of her mother's death, Estrella had learned to cook and sew and look after her father. They were very happy in their little white house that was surrounded by Naranja trees. Every morning, except Sunday, Señorita Estrella went to her window to wave to Zonta when he passed by on his prancing Caballo.

And Zonta made his Caballo prance a little more when he saw her at the window. This made Estrella sigh happily. And when she sighed Naranjas fell from the Naranja trees.

Fourth Capitulo

Y Estoy Amando. El esta Amando. (This means
that Zonta and Estrella were in love. This is a
secret, so it is written in Spanish.)

*

*

*

*

*

*

*

*

*

(One day they hoped to get married in Father Potelo's little white church. This is also a secret.)

Fifth Capitulo

IN the evenings when the moonlight painted the town a pale yellow, and when strange shadows stretched across the streets, Zonta climbed the long spiral staircase that went to the top of the old Castillo. From a small castellated balcony he looked down on El Zapato. In the market-place the waters of the slim fountain shimmered in the moonlight. Here and there were blobs of yellow light. Wisps of lazy smoke curled from chimney-pots. And under those round, black shapes that seemed to glide down the streets like floating saucers were fat little legs and bodies, all waddling towards the Paradiso Café. From the brightly lit Café came lively music and laughter. A musician was strumming on a Spanish guitar and singing a song about Naranjas.

"Strum, strum, strum. . . .
Oh, I will grow Naranjas, Naranjas, Naranjas,
  I will grow Naranjas,
And give them to my love.
Oh! Oh! Naranjas, sweet, sweet Naranjas,
  I will grow Naranjas,
And give them to my love."

As Zonta listened, the pear-shaped doors of Father Potelo's church opened and Señorita

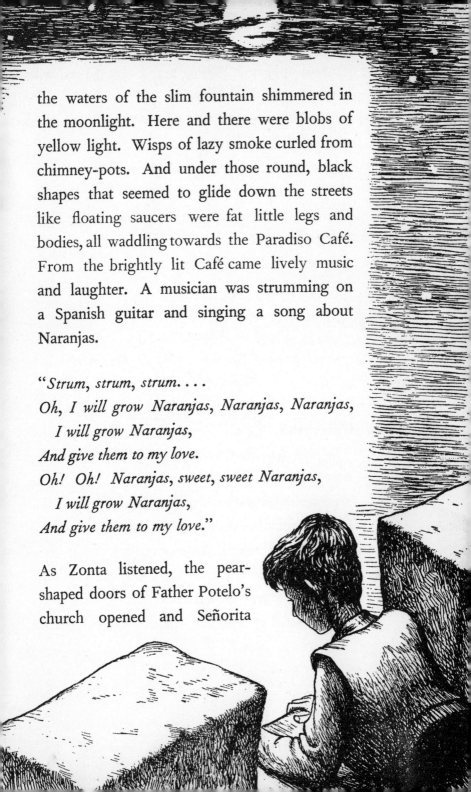

Estrella appeared. Seeing her, Zonta danced with joy and waved excitedly.

Looking neither to left nor right, her eyes always on Zonta at the top of the Castillo, Estrella hurried down the cobbled street to a favourite shadow that waited beside the wall of the Castillo. For a moment or two she stood there while Zonta lowered a rope with a note attached to the end. She read the note at once.

To Estrella
I love you.
Buenas Noches ... Hasta Mañana
From Zonta. No. 57.

This meant, "Good night.... Until to-morrow." The note was the fifty-seventh he had sent her by rope. She smiled and then hurried away to the little white house that was surrounded by Naranja trees. From her balcony, the balcony that was decorated with pink geraniums, she waved good night and sighed. If only she could speak to him. If only he would speak to her. Unfortunately ...

But at that moment the town clock struck

eight. Estrella closed her bedroom window. Zonta descended the long spiral staircase to his four-poster bed.

Buenas noches!

Sixth Capitulo

ALTHOUGH Dona Barcelo was very beautiful, she was also very sad. She was sad because her son had never been able to talk. For five years the great Doctor Bomba had tried to coax Zonta's tongue to talk. He had tickled it with a feather, painted it with iodine, and finally he had it soaking in pure honey for a whole week. All in vain.

"It's too comfortable," cried the exasperated Doctor. "If it were my tongue I'd keep it wagging until it shouted for help."

The obedient Zonta wagged his tongue night after night, week after week. All in vain.

"He will never be a politician," said Bomba.

"He will be a Matador like me. You don't need a tongue to be a Matador," said Don Barcelo.

So Zonta looked disappointed and thought of the fierce bulls. His mother remembered an ancient Spanish proverb.

"Silence is golden. You will be rich, my son," she whispered.

Zonta rolled his eyes to please his mother. Secretly he felt very sad. He would never be able to speak to Estrella!

"Oh dear," he thought. "I hope she won't be too disappointed."

Like his beautiful mother, Zonta kept his sadness a secret. They both smiled, and they both appeared to be very happy.

Seventh Capitulo

WHILE the famous Matador grew smooth, black side-whiskers, and while the people of El Zapato grew millions of sweet Naranjas, Señorita Estrella grew more beautiful every day. She also worked very hard in her little white house. Each year she learned how to make a new soup. This year it was Soya Bean soup. This made her learned father, the schoolmaster, look forward to a New Year and to a New Soup.

Every evening Estrella stood on a stool in the kitchen and stirred a steaming soup of Soya

Beans. Orquesta, the cat, sat at her feet and sang a song of Naranjas. Sitting in a corner of the exquisitely tiled fireplace sat Father Potelo. He was very fat and jolly, and often came to dinner. While he waited for his favourite soup he played a merry little tune on his piccolo.

When the clock on the wall said six-thirty, Father Potelo put his piccolo in his pocket and tasted the soup.

"*Excellentio!* Tell your Papa that dinner is ready," he called through the steam.

Estrella took up a pencil.

"Dinner is ready, Papa," she wrote, and then gave the note to her father, who was in the garden reading history under a Naranja tree.

"*Bueno!*" he cried. "I am very hungry after journeying round the world with Columbus."

They all dined in the kitchen at a long, fat-legged table that had a large loaf and a fat jug of wine in the centre. They ate their soup from wooden bowls and liked it.

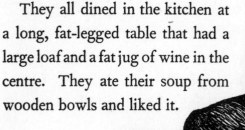

Eighth Capitulo

IF you asked Father Potelo if everybody was happy in El Zapato, he would laugh and laugh and shake like a barrel rolling down a hill.

"*Si . . si . . . SI*," he would say. "Everybody is very happy in El Zapato." But in Father Potelo's church—the church that had a Campana above its pear-shaped doors, and where all the windows were of stained-glass with portraits of saints in purple robes—there lodged an old broom called Dona Bella. She lived in a cupboard that had a large keyhole. Through the keyhole she could spy upon her enemies and see them swarm over the pews, over the pulpit, over the floor, and even up the candles, where they delighted to climb and warm their hands against the flames.

"THE COCKROACHES!" screeched Dona Bella. "CHARGE!"

The next moment she would spring from her cupboard and go swishing and swooshing, chasing and screeching down the aisle.

"GET OUT! COME OFF THOSE PEWS... SWISH.. SWOOSH.. SWISH.. OUT!"

Scrittle and scrattle, tumble and bundle, jumble and mumble. "*Cuidado ... Cuidado!*" Bump ... thump! Swish, swash, swoosh. Topple and turnover. "Run ... run! It's Dona Bella the BROOM!"

And this happened every night. And every night the Cockroaches ran to their Leader.

"Don Domino!... Don Domino!" they chorused.

Don Domino had white spots on his shiny brown back. He lived in a table drawer in the vestry. He was very kind and gentle— even wise. He peered from the drawer.

"Yes, my friends?" he asked.

"Why doesn't that old broom leave us in peace?"

Don Domino blinked, frowned, scratched his head, then shook his head.

"I don't know—yet. But I shall find an answer. Just leave me in peace. Be patient. There's an answer to every question."

And with a smile he waved to them.

"Take care of yourselves," he croaked. "Listen for the latch on the cupboard."

Don Domino returned to the drawer where Father Potelo kept his old sermons. Page after page, along every written line, Don Domino marched through the sermons.

"The answer's here. I know it is," he mumbled.

And so he marched in his private quest.

If you asked Father Potelo if there were Cockroaches in his church he would laugh and laugh and shake like a barrel rolling down a cobbled street.

"*Si . . . si . . . si.* There are Cockroaches in my church. They, too, are happy. Everybody is happy in El Zapato."

And now you know that nothing really exciting ever happened in El Zapato. It was a very peaceful town.

On Sunday El Zapato was especially peaceful. Only Father Potelo made a noise when he rang the Campana in the Belfry.

Once in the morning. *Ding dong.*

Twice in the evening. *Ding dong. Ding dong.*

And when the people heard the bell they all went to the little white church at the end of the main street. Dona Bella saw them enter and she saw them leave. The Cockroaches saw nothing at all. On Sunday they slept all day.

Ninth Capitulo

BUT one summer's evening when all the townsfolk had gone to bed something exciting did happen.

From the moonlit Campo a fat Caballero rode into the town at a furious gallop. The clippety clop of the Caballo's hooves echoed and echoed on the cobbled streets. People ran to their doors and windows in night attire. The whole town awakened suddenly. The Caballero rode so hard that he passed El Zapato in a flash. He returned and drew rein in front of the huge doors of the Castillo.

"It is Señor Martillo the Bull-grower," cried the people.

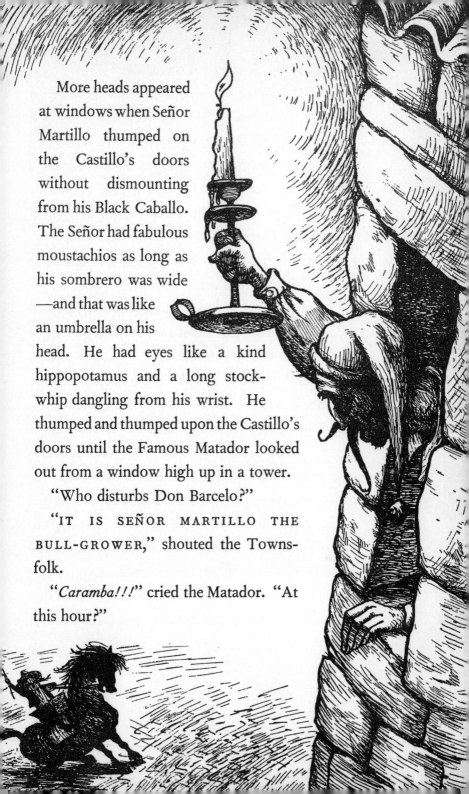

More heads appeared at windows when Señor Martillo thumped on the Castillo's doors without dismounting from his Black Caballo. The Señor had fabulous moustachios as long as his sombrero was wide —and that was like an umbrella on his head. He had eyes like a kind hippopotamus and a long stock-whip dangling from his wrist. He thumped and thumped upon the Castillo's doors until the Famous Matador looked out from a window high up in a tower.

"Who disturbs Don Barcelo?"

"IT IS SEÑOR MARTILLO THE BULL-GROWER," shouted the Towns-folk.

"*Caramba!!!*" cried the Matador. "At this hour?"

"YES," shouted the Townsfolk.

Half asleep, the Matador shook himself and then became wide awake. He lit a candle and hurried down a spiral staircase to open the Castillo's great front doors. He received his visitor in a bright red dressing-gown and a pair of yellow carpet slippers. Holding the candle above his head, Don Barcelo glared at Señor Martillo.

"You thump at a late hour, Señor," cried the Matador with dignified annoyance. "*Adelante!*"

Señor Martillo followed Don Barcelo into the Banqueting Hall on horseback, because he forgot to leave his Caballo outside.

"What's up?" snapped the Matador, pushing the Black Caballo off his rich Indian carpet.

"I have grown a bull that is fiercer than a tiger," cried Señor Martillo. "He has horns as sharp as needles and a neck like a pillar-box. He is *Terrrrrifico*. I have called him El Sarten the Terrrrrifico Bull. He is *magnifico*."

"*Caramba!!!*" cried Don Barcelo, not a little disturbed. "How many tons does he weigh?"

"Three tons! *Terrrifico!*" shouted Señor Martillo and struck the Banqueting Hall table with his stock-whip. "Three tons and a quarter. *Magnifico!* What sport for you, Don Barcelo! All Spain will turn out to see you kill him. I have never grown a fiercer, fatter or more dangerous bull in my life." And Señor Martillo smiled because *he* knew he wouldn't have to fight the bull.

"*Gorrah! Dios Mio. Caramba!*"

Don Barcelo didn't look at all cheerful. On the other hand, the fat Bull-grower appeared to be in the best of humour. He cracked his long stock-whip and laughed and rode round the Banqueting Hall table on his fine Black Caballo.

"Has the bull killed anyone yet?" asked the Matador.

"*Estou com pressa,*" replied Martillo in Portuguese.

"Why do you speak Portuguese?" cried Don Barcelo angrily.

"I am in a hurry. My horse is Portuguese," mumbled the Bull-grower. "I must go."

"*Alto,*" cried the Matador. "How many men has this bull killed?"

"Just two, Señor Matador. Only two—not three."

Don Barcelo looked *very* unhappy. He knew that if there were two of anything there were bound to be three.

"*Gorrah!* He must be VERY fierce."

"El Sarten is *tremendosio*. He will give a wonderful performance in the arena. What a friend I am to give you the best bull in Spain to fight."

"You are TOO kind, Señor Martillo...TOO KIND!"

"*Adios*," cried the Bull-grower, and he rode out of the back door to save opening the front door. "*Adios*."

Disturbed and distraught, Don Barcelo rested his head on his elbows on the Banqueting Hall table. The more he thought about El Sarten the bigger the bull seemed to grow.

"Oh, pickle me piccolo," he mumbled.

Suddenly he jumped to his feet. In the candle-light his shadow jumped to the wall and danced. Don Barcelo had begun to practise for his fight with the bull. He turned this way and that. He thrust here and there. He growled and grumbled, jumped and dodged, turned and twisted, and cried,

"Oley . . . oley . . . grrrrrrrrh . . . Oley . . . grrrrrrrrrh!"

The noise soon brought Zonta to the Minstrels' Gallery which overlooked the Banqueting Hall. An expression of great astonishment spread over his face as he watched his famous Papa fighting an imaginary bull. The noise also brought beautiful Mama to the scene. When she saw what was going on she lit another candle and reprimanded her husband kindly.

"You will strain your eyes with only one candle, my dear."

"Oley . . . oley . . . grrrrrrrrr. Thank you, my love. Grrrrrrrr," said the Matador.

"*Buenas noches,*" said Dona Barcelo, and she returned to her four-poster as if nothing unusual was astir.

Zonta also retired. But before he got back into his four-poster he turned the pictures surrounding his bed to the wall. He didn't want to dream of bulls. He wanted to dream of Estrella in the little white house that was surrounded by Naranja trees.

Tenth Capitulo

THERE was tremendous excitement in El Zapato when the people heard of the Terrrrifico Bull. They danced and sang and forgot to sleep during the day. Whenever they saw Don Barcelo on his beautiful Caballo they cheered louder than ever and threw their hats—or whatever they had on their heads—into the air. The boys dreamed of becoming famous Matadors. The girls dreamed of marrying brave Matadors. What is more, El Sarten became as famous as the Famous Matador in one night!

Señorita Estrella was also very excited. She took up a watering-can and watered her roses in preparation for the *Corrida de Toros*. Then she took out her mother's mantilla and a rare old Spanish shawl of beautiful design. She tried them on and admired herself in the mirror. Everybody would be going to the Bullfight—even Father Potelo.

While everybody was so happy and excited, Don Barcelo began to knit frowns. He felt very trembly. The more he thought of Sarten the Terrrrrrifico Bull the more trembly he felt. Even Famous Matadors find it very difficult to be brave ALL the time.

High up in the Castillo, Zonta and his mother remained very calm. They didn't want Don Barcelo to know that they were at all worried. At meal-times they smiled cosy smiles and behaved as if everything would turn out for the best—or even better.

But one evening, soon after midnight had

chimed, Don Barcelo was suddenly awakened by the bellowing of a bull in the Campo. He shot out of his four-poster like a jack-in-the-box and trembled. When he had finished trembling he lit a candle and put on his yellow carpet slippers. Then he tip-toed down the spiral staircase to the Great Hall. There he put on his wide sombrero and threw a magnificent red-and-gold cape over his night attire. Lighting his way with a candle, Don Barcelo stole out from the Old Castillo and tip-toed down the cobbled street towards Father Potelo's church. He was off to say a little prayer for himself.

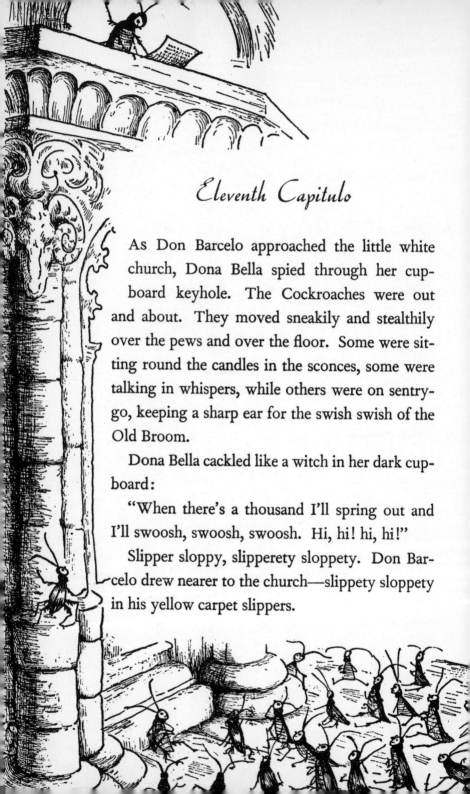

Eleventh Capitulo

As Don Barcelo approached the little white church, Dona Bella spied through her cupboard keyhole. The Cockroaches were out and about. They moved sneakily and stealthily over the pews and over the floor. Some were sitting round the candles in the sconces, some were talking in whispers, while others were on sentry-go, keeping a sharp ear for the swish swish of the Old Broom.

Dona Bella cackled like a witch in her dark cupboard:

"When there's a thousand I'll spring out and I'll swoosh, swoosh, swoosh. Hi, hi! hi, hi!"

Slipper sloppy, slipperety sloppety. Don Barcelo drew nearer to the church—slippety sloppety in his yellow carpet slippers.

Don Domino came tearing out of the vestry waving a piece of paper in the air.

"I've found it," he cried joyously. "I've found it at LAST."

And like Father Potelo when he had something important to say, Don Domino climbed into the pulpit and said:

"Pray be seated, my friends."

So the Cockroaches sat in front of the pulpit and looked up at their leader like the people of El Zapato looked up at Father Potelo—with wide-open eyes and ears.

Don Domino walked to and fro on the ledge of the pulpit where Father Potelo rested his elbows. He paused and smiled triumphantly.

"I have found it at LAST, my friends. After years of searching I can now give you the answer you all desire. The answer to your question: Why doesn't Dona Bella leave you in peace? I found it in one of Father Potelo's sermons. I shall read it to you."

The Cockroaches sat closer. Some

cupped their ears in order to hear more clearly.

Dona Bella's spying eye wriggled round the keyhole. What was going on out there? She couldn't see a Cockroach. They had vanished. Slowly, little by little, she lifted the latch of the cupboard.

Don Domino began to read from the paper in his hand.

"If we want peace in our lives we must learn to love our enemies," he said, and smiled. "That is the answer to your question."

The Cockroaches frowned and looked from one to the other.

"You mean . . . ?" they gasped.

"Yes," said Don Domino. "We must try and love Dona Bella. We must pray for her to be kind."

"Pray for that rickety old stick," croaked a Cockroach. "I won't for one."

"Neither will I," said another.

"Nor I."

Don Domino held up his hands in dismay.

"My friends . . . listen to me . . . listen. . . ."

And while the Cockroaches argued and shouted
Dona Bella got ready to spring from her cupboard. She was just about to spring when the
church doors opened and Don Barcelo entered.
He came tiptoeing down the aisle, his sombrero
in one hand, the candle in the
other. Dona Bella fell back
into her cupboard.

Placing his candle on
the altar, Don Barcelo

knelt in prayer. The Cockroaches fled to the pulpit and listened. It soon became very plain to all that Don Barcelo had no intention of praying for anyone except himself.

"Why doesn't he pray for Sarten the Bull?" asked a Cockroach. "That's his enemy."

"Yes, why doesn't he?" asked another.

There was a look of great disappointment on Don Domino's face as he listened to the grumblings of his friends. Unable to stand it any longer, Don Domino set off down the pulpit.

"Where are you going?" cried the Cockroaches.

"I'm going to give Don Barcelo the message," he called over his shoulder.

Off he went along the stone floor, jumping over the cracks, taking short cuts under the pews until he reached the yellow carpet slippers. And at that moment came tragedy. Don Barcelo rose suddenly to his feet and trampled Don Domino underfoot. Turning away from the altar, Don Barcelo tiptoed away down the aisle in his yellow carpet slippers. The church doors opened and closed.

"Don Domino, Don Domino," wept the Cockroaches. "Oh, Don Domino."

The Cockroaches flocked to their dying leader.

"Not to worry, my friends," said Don Domino in a weak voice. "My own fault."

"Is there nothing we can do?"

"Pray for Dona Bella, my friends. Pray for her to be kind and gentle," whispered Don Domino.

And as the Cockroaches gathered round Don Domino, Dona Bella stole down the aisle looking for her enemies. Reaching the last pew, she halted abruptly. There they were! What a wonderful opportunity to swoosh and make one clean sweep! "One, two and I'll swoop," she said. But something quite extraordinary was taking place. The Cockroaches were not only praying for Don Barcelo and Sarten the Bull, they were also praying for Dona Bella.

"*Dios mio!*" cried the Broom. "They're praying for me!"

Astounded, Dona Bella flopped into a pew, unable to believe her own ears. Instead of swooping upon the Cockroaches she watched them carry Don Domino back to the vestry.

Twelfth Capitulo

AT one minute to one, soon after Don Domino had passed on to his Happy Abode, and when the Famous Matador was only half-way down the cobbled street, El Sarten the Terrrrifico Bull bellowed a great bellow across the Campo. Don Barcelo's hair stood up in fright; his wide sombrero shivered on his head, his candle shook in his hand as he trembled at the sound. Then came another sound—the sound of a galloping Caballo: "Clippety clop clop clop clop clop." Nearer and nearer, louder and louder: "Clippety clop clop CLOP!" Along the Campo trail Señor Martillo rode his fine Black Caballo. In a flash he passed the town, and the wind from his speed put out Don Barcelo's candlelight.

"Whoa!" cried the fine Black Caballo in Portuguese, and reared up on his haunches. "We've left Don Barcelo in the dark."

"*Sinto muito*," said Señor Martillo, which meant that he was very sorry. "Let us return to El Zapato."

In a flash of speed they passed Don Barcelo again, and the sparks from the Caballo's iron shoes lit the Matador's candle.

"Whoa," cried Señor Martillo in Spanish, and he reared up in the stirrups to pull his speeding steed to a halt. "Whoa, my silly fellow."

By now all the Townsfolk were awake, and they peered from their windows and saw Don Barcelo standing in a pool of candlelight. They also saw Señor Martillo on his Black Caballo trippety trotting down the street towards the Matador.

"Why do you put my candle out and then in?" cried Don Barcelo.

"*Pardonico*, señor," said the Bull-grower. "But I came in a hurry to get an aspirin for Sarten the Terrrrifico—he can't sleep."

"Why can't he sleep?" cried the Matador, growing alarmed.

"He has been dreaming of Little Cockroaches. He is very upset."

And as he spoke Sarten bellowed another great bellow across the Campo. Without waiting to hear any more, Don Barcelo fled down the street, and the wind from his speed blew his candle out and then it blew his cape out. The great doors of the old Castillo opened and closed. Taking another lighted candle from the sconce in the Great Hall, Don Barcelo continued swiftly up the spiral staircase. And all the Townsfolk watched him as he passed from window to window with his light, climbing higher and higher until he reached the last window.

"He's gone to bed," said the Townsfolk.

"And he didn't even say good night," neighed the fine Black Caballo.

"*Buenas noches*," called the Townsfolk as they, too, went to bed.

Señor Martillo yawned.

"*Boas noites*," he cried and turned his steed about and stole away across the Campo with a quiet clippety cloppety clippety clip clip clip ... until he fell asleep in the saddle.

"Sleep well, Master," said the Black Caballo. "I wish I was in your stirrups."

And with a long-drawn-out yawn and a loud brrrrrrrrh, the Black Caballo closed one eye. He kept the other open to find the way home.

Thirteenth Capitulo

MORE alarmed than ever, Don Barcelo sat on his four-poster bed and played a flute. He played in a slow elegiac tempo, and with sentimental execution. This is what he played:—

Las flores del romero,
Nina Isabel,
Hoy son flores azules,
Mañana seran miel.

When this is translated into English it means:—

The flowers of the rosemary,
  Little Isabel,
To-day are blue flowers,
  To-morrow they will be honey.

So you can guess what was on the Matador's
mind.

Fourteenth Capitulo

AND SO, Don Barcelo got into his four-poster bed. As soon as his head touched the pillow the Town Hall clock began to strike. On the stroke of one, Don Barcelo turned over on his left shoulder. On the stroke of two, he turned over on his right shoulder. On the stroke of three, he sat up in bed. The moonlight lit his round room in the tower.

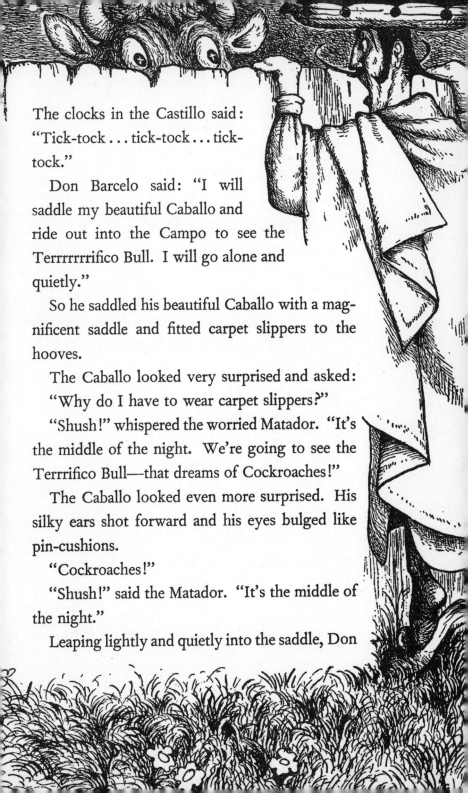

The clocks in the Castillo said: "Tick-tock ... tick-tock ... tick-tock."

Don Barcelo said: "I will saddle my beautiful Caballo and ride out into the Campo to see the Terrrrrrrifico Bull. I will go alone and quietly."

So he saddled his beautiful Caballo with a magnificent saddle and fitted carpet slippers to the hooves.

The Caballo looked very surprised and asked: "Why do I have to wear carpet slippers?"

"Shush!" whispered the worried Matador. "It's the middle of the night. We're going to see the Terrrifico Bull—that dreams of Cockroaches!"

The Caballo looked even more surprised. His silky ears shot forward and his eyes bulged like pin-cushions.

"Cockroaches!"

"Shush!" said the Matador. "It's the middle of the night."

Leaping lightly and quietly into the saddle, Don

Barcelo spurred his Caballo into a gallop and galloped away.

Cloomfetty cloomf ... cloomfetty cloomf ... cloomf ... cloomf.

The muffled sound of galloping hooves echoed quietly across the moonlit Campo.

In the round stockyard on Señor Martillo's Farm, El Sarten the Terrrrrifico Bull snortled and chumfled.

"Cloomfetty cloomf ... cloomfetty cloomf."

At the sound Sarten pricked up his ears. He listened. Nearer and nearer rode Don Barcelo until ...

"Whoa!"

The Famous Matador dismounted within a yard or two of the round, brick stockyard.

"Wait here," whispered Don Barcelo to his beautiful Caballo, and then tiptoed towards the stockyard wall. At the same time El Sarten tiptoed to the stockyard wall. As he looked out, a wide sombrero rose up before him like a growing mushroom. Then a pair of eyes appeared. When Don Barcelo stared, he stared into the saucer-like eyes of the Terrrifico Bull. He saw himself blink. He saw his wide sombrero rise above his head.

"Pickle me piccolo," he gasped.

And then a strange, gruff voice said:

"Who are you?"

"I'm the Famous Matador of El Zapato."

"Don Barcelo!"

"Y-y-y-y-y-yes," stammered Don Barcelo, and his wide sombrero rose higher and higher when he heard the bull talk.

"I have a message for you, Señor Matador. A message from a Little Cockroach who died in Father Potelo's church early this morning. He came to see me in a dream and asked me . . ."

Don Barcelo's eyes opened wider and wider. His wide sombrero rose higher and higher. He turned and fled.

"Hey . . . come back!" bellowed Sarten. "I have a message for you, Señor Matador. . . . SEÑOR!"

CLOOMFETTY CLOOMF CLOOMFETTY CLOOMF . . . cloomfetty cloomf cloomf . . .

"That's Bull's MAD. He dreams of Cockroaches!" he cried as he galloped home.

Fifteenth Capitulo

For a whole week Don Barcelo remained in the old Castillo and counted the days. He was very worried. Every time he thought of El Sarten the Terrrrrrrifico Bull he trembled. And every time he trembled he wrote a letter:

"Dear Señor Martillo,

         Please cancel the Bullfight. I don't feel very well. . . ."

A few minutes later he wrote another letter:

"Dear Señor Martillo,

D ON'T cancel the Bullfight. I feel a lot better to-day. . . ."

Of course, he never posted the letters. Nor did he show them to anyone. He was too proud to admit that he was afraid. Besides, he was a Famous Matador, and everybody expected him to be very brave—even Zonta.

In the round, brick stockyard on the Spanish Farm, Sarten waited impatiently to meet Don Barcelo again. He felt that he would never be really happy until he had delivered the Little Cockroach's message. As each day passed he grew more impatient.

Then came the great day—the day of the Bullfight.

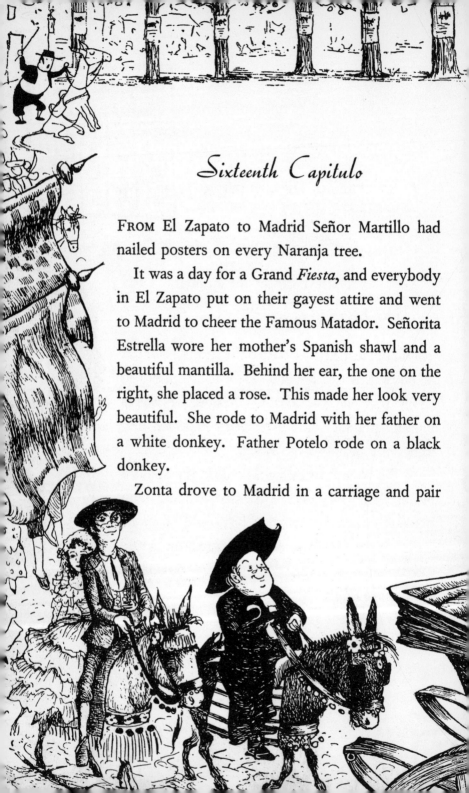

Sixteenth Capitulo

FROM El Zapato to Madrid Señor Martillo had nailed posters on every Naranja tree.

It was a day for a Grand *Fiesta*, and everybody in El Zapato put on their gayest attire and went to Madrid to cheer the Famous Matador. Señorita Estrella wore her mother's Spanish shawl and a beautiful mantilla. Behind her ear, the one on the right, she placed a rose. This made her look very beautiful. She rode to Madrid with her father on a white donkey. Father Potelo rode on a black donkey.

Zonta drove to Madrid in a carriage and pair

with his Papa and Mama and Doctor Bomba.
When the people saw them they cried out aloud:

"There goes Don Barcelo and his beautiful
wife. Hurrah!"

"And that's his son sitting beside him. Hurrah!"

The beautiful Dona Isabella Verano Primavera
smiled and waved to the crowds. Zonta
gave little nods to right and left, but
Don Barcelo sat very straight, deep in his
own particular thoughts. His
wife nudged him.

"The people are cheering you," she said.

"Cockroaches! He dreams of Cockroaches," said the Famous Matador.

Dona Isabella stared at her husband in amazement.

"What odd things you say!" she said.

"It is odd, isn't it?" he answered.

In reply his wife said:

"Everyone knows best where the shoe pinches him." And turning to the crowds, Dona Isabella smiled and waved again.

On another road El Sarten the Terrrrifico Bull travelled in a lion's cage that had been borrowed from a Spanish circus. When the people saw him they gasped.

"He must be the strongest and ugliest bull that has ever been born," they cried.

Sarten didn't mind being referred to as an ugly bull because he had a beautiful message to give to Don Barcelo. He ignored the crowds and recited Don Domino's message to himself. Señor Martillo rode beside the lion's cage on his fine Black Caballo that had been born in Portugal.

"*Es un toro magnifico.* . . . *Y que fuerza tiene!*"
he shouted.

"Why don't you speak in Portuguese?" said
the Black Caballo, "so that we can ALL under-
stand."

"Oh, you silly Caballo!" whispered Señor
Martillo. "I only said Sarten was a magnificent
bull and very strong."

"Oh, I see. Sorry."

An hour later Sarten was in his stall waiting to
be released into the Bullring. As he waited he
grew more and more impatient. The vast arena
outside was crowded. The spectators shouted and
cheered:

"LONG LIVE DON BARCELO!"

Then a trumpet sounded.

"TARAH . . . TARAH DE DADDI AH"

The Grand Parade of Matadors, Picadores and
Banderilleros entered the arena. Dressed in
magnificent clothes of red and blue and gold, they
marched smartly across the hot, yellow sand. As
they marched they acknowledged the cheering
crowds with little flicks of their hands.

"BRAVO, DON BARCELO!"

Zonta clapped his hands. Señorita Estrella threw a rose into the ring, the one from behind her right ear.

When the Matadors and Picadores and Banderilleros had taken up their positions the trumpet sounded a second time.

"TA RAH TA RAH DE DADDIA AH."

Sarten's stable door was thrown open. The enormous Bull, who had the strength of ten and a neck as thick as a pillar-box, romped into the arena like a gambolling lamb. But so fierce and ugly did he appear that all the people gasped in horror:

"G-G-G-GORSH!"

At the far end of the arena Don Barcelo trembled.

"P-p-p-pickle-me-p-p-p-piccolo," he stammered, and the bright vermilion cape he held in his hands shook like a sheet in a wind.

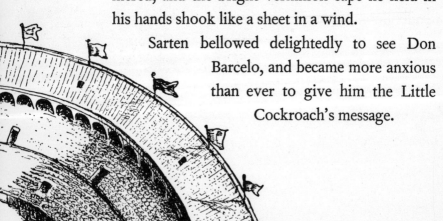

Sarten bellowed delightedly to see Don Barcelo, and became more anxious than ever to give him the Little Cockroach's message.

Forthwith he set off in all haste.

The ground shook as he romped to-wards the Matador, gathering speed as he went. "*Cuidado . . . Cuidado!*" yelled the crowds. "LOOK OUT!"

Faster and faster went the Terrrrrifico Bull.

"I have a message for you," he cried.

But so great was his speed, and because he had no brakes to halt his thundering rompetty romp, within a jiffy Sarten reached the Matador—and could not stop. Up came his horns, up went Don Barcelo into the blue sky. Higher and higher he went until the arena looked like a beehive with the middle out. When Don Barcelo looked down he saw the spectators looking up, and they ALL looked surprised.

Believing that the Famous Matador was some-
where in the arena, Sarten ran hither and thither
peering over barricades.

"Where is he?" bellowed the Terrifico Bull.

And all the spectators pointed to the blue sky.

"GORSH!" cried Sarten.

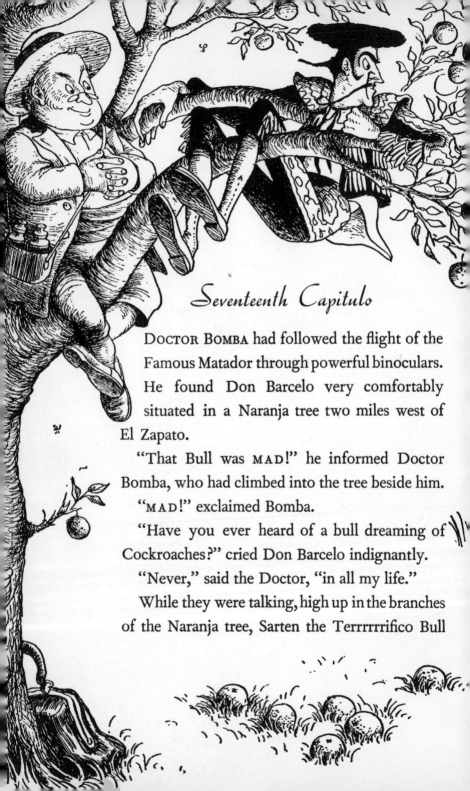

Seventeenth Capitulo

DOCTOR BOMBA had followed the flight of the
Famous Matador through powerful binoculars.
He found Don Barcelo very comfortably
situated in a Naranja tree two miles west of
El Zapato.

"That Bull was MAD!" he informed Doctor
Bomba, who had climbed into the tree beside him.

"MAD!" exclaimed Bomba.

"Have you ever heard of a bull dreaming of
Cockroaches?" cried Don Barcelo indignantly.

"Never," said the Doctor, "in all my life."

While they were talking, high up in the branches
of the Naranja tree, Sarten the Terrrrrifico Bull

passed by. He was accompanied by a Brass Band and cheering admirers.

"Congratulations!" shouted the Matador. "I hope you're pleased with yourself."

Sarten pricked up his ears. He turned this way and that in the lion's cage.

"Don Barcelo . . . where are you?"

But at that moment the man with the big drum went "BOOM BOOM BOOM". The Trumpeters went: "Ta rah tahrah de daddia ah de dah". The cheering people cheered louder than ever.

"DON BARCELO!" bellowed Sarten again.

"He's quite mad," said the Famous Matador.

And from the Naranja tree, Don Barcelo and Doctor Bomba watched the Lion's cage out of sight.

Eighteenth Capitulo

AFTER his undignified exit from the Bullring, Don Barcelo lost all his fame and prestige. He was no longer referred to as the Famous Matador. The people of El Zapato nicknamed him "The Pancake", and whenever he appeared in the street they stood and laughed. This made Don Barcelo very unhappy and very ashamed, so he retired to the top of the old Castillo and grew hairy with sorrow.

His smooth, black side-whiskers curled away from his aristocratic nose and grew into a beard.

Dona Isabella became very frightened when she met her husband on the spiral staircase, so she decided to use another spiral staircase.

Poor Zonta was also very unhappy. He no longer rode past the little white house that was surrounded by Naranja trees on his beautiful Caballo. Every morning he walked with his mother on her spiral staircase. In the afternoons he walked with his father on his spiral staircase. Zonta was very fond of his parents, and he hoped that they would soon be happy and use the same spiral staircase again.

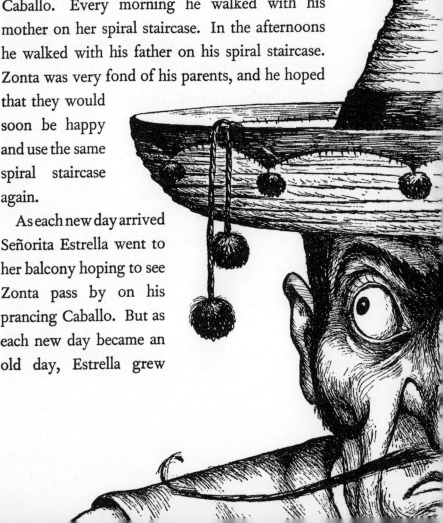

As each new day arrived Señorita Estrella went to her balcony hoping to see Zonta pass by on his prancing Caballo. But as each new day became an old day, Estrella grew very sad, so she wept into the steaming Soya Bean Soup. This made Father Potelo and the schoolmaster and Orquesta the Cat very hungry because the soup became very thin.

And although Sarten had become very famous, he was the unhappiest Bull that had ever bellowed across a Spanish Campo. He grew sadder and sadder, and refused to eat.

"If only I could give the Little Cockroach's message to Don Barcelo I'd be the happiest bull in the world," he said to himself.

Each day he looked over the stockyard wall for Don Barcelo. And each day he was disappointed.

Even Señor Martillo grew despondent. He no longer spoke to his fine Black Caballo in Portuguese, nor did he crack his long thonged stockwhip in merry jest. He had been all over Spain offering large prizes to anyone who would challenge Sarten the Terrrrrifico. Not one volunteer came forward. Then, one day. . . .

Nineteenth Capitulo

THEN, one day when Don Barcelo's beard was so long that he was continually tripping himself up on his spiral staircase, Zonta wrote a letter, not to Estrella, but to his father.

10. AM.

The Old Castillo
El Zapato

Dear Papa.
May I fight
Sarten the Bull?

your loving son
Zonta.

> The Old Castillo
> El Zapato
> 10.15.Am.
>
> Dear Mama
> I dont want
> to be a sailor.
> I want to be a
> Matador like
> Papa. May I?
> Your loving Son,
> Zonta. X.

This is the letter Zonta
wrote to his mother.

When Don Barcelo read the letter he
hurried, tripped, tumbled and rolled
down the spiral staircase to say "NO!"

Having said "NO!" very firmly, he
hurried back up the spiral staircase to
be sad again.

But Zonta was very determined, so
he wrote the letter to his
mother, which you can see at
the top of the page.

Dona Barcelo read the letter in
her boudoir, where she had
gone to be frightened. Proudly
she descended her spiral staircase and said "Yes".

Zonta then wrote this letter to his father.

> 10.20 A.m.   The old Castillo
> El Zapato
>
> Dear Papa
> Mama
> Says "Yes"
> your loving son
> Zonta

Now, Don Barcelo was a very wise and courteous gentleman who never argued with ladies, so he wrote to his son from the top of the old Castillo.

> 12.15. P.m.   The Old Castillo
> El Zapato.
>
> My brave Son.
> If your Mother
> Says "Yes" we must
> all say Yes.
> You make me very
> proud.
> Your loving Papa
> Don Navidad Lunes Barcelo

Zonta answered his
father's letter like this

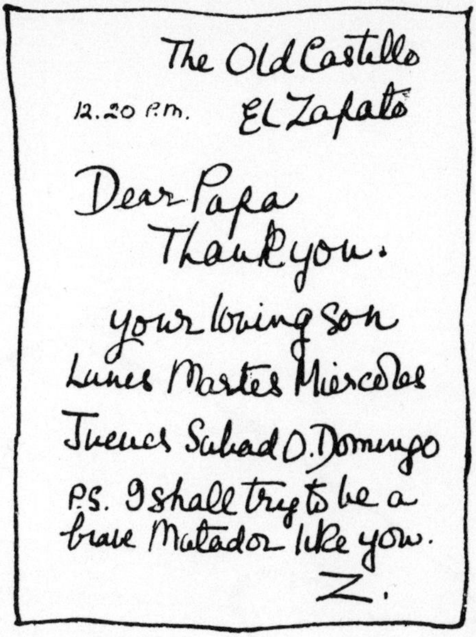

> The Old Castillo
> 12.20 P.m. El Zapato
>
> Dear Papa
>   Thank you.
>   your loving son
> Lunes Martes Miercoles
> Jueves Sabado Domingo
> P.S. I shall try to be a
> brave Matador like you.
>   Z.

The following morning the Postmaster of El
Zapato rode across the Campo on a red horse that
was marked "ROYAL MAIL". In his pocket the
Postmaster carried a letter which was addressed
to—

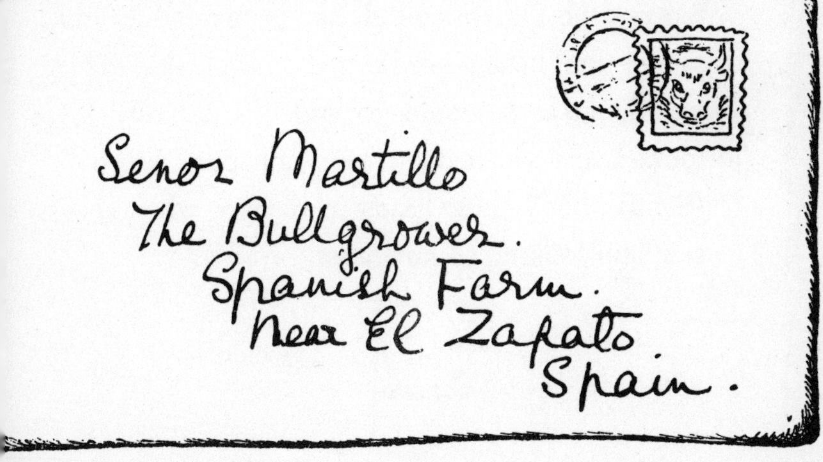

> Senor Martillo
> The Bullgrower.
> Spanish Farm.
> near El Zapato.
>   Spain.

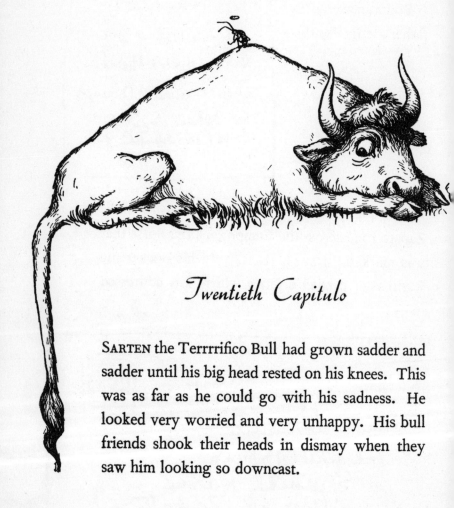

Twentieth Capitulo

SARTEN the Terrrrifico Bull had grown sadder and sadder until his big head rested on his knees. This was as far as he could go with his sadness. He looked very worried and very unhappy. His bull friends shook their heads in dismay when they saw him looking so downcast.

"He's never been the same since he dreamt of the Little Cockroach," they said. "Don't think he'll last long. Pity, and him so famous."

And just as Sarten was about to give up all hope of ever delivering the Little Cock-roach's message, the Postmaster of El Zapato came jog-trotting across the Campo on his red horse.

"Jogetty jiggety jogetty trottety trot trot. I've gottety a lettety in my pocketty jogetty trottety. Gee uppetty."

Sarten raised his weary head and looked.

There was a whoop of delight and a crack crack crack of a long thonged stock-whip echoed over the Campo. Señor Martillo had suddenly become jolly again. The Farmhands cheered and the Postmaster cheered, but the fine Black Caballo from Portugal looked puzzled.

"What's up?" he asked in Portuguese.

And Señor Martillo read him the letter he had just received.

> "The Old Castillo
> El Zapato.
>
> Dear Señor Martillo,
>   I will fight Sarten the Terrrifico Bull.
> Mama says 'Yes'. Papa is very proud.
>   Signed, Zonta Barcelo, son of the Famous Matador, Don Barcelo."

The Bull-grower threw his wide sombrero into the air.

"*Magnifico*. I will call him the Little Matador."

"Well, well, well, I'll eat my saddle," said the fine Black Caballo. "That is news."

It was the best news Sarten had heard for many a long day. He threw away his sadness and then bellowed a great bellow.

"I'll give the Little Cockroach's message to Don Barcelo's son. That's what I will do."

And so, Sarten grew happier and happier, and each day he recited Don Domino's message to himself to make sure he remembered it.

Twenty-first Capitulo

"TAH-RAH...TAH RAH ...TAH RAH DE DADDIAH DAH!"

Señor Martillo sat on his fine Black Caballo in the market-place at El Zapato and blew down his long winded trumpet in Spanish. The horrible noise brought all the townsfolk hurrying from their houses to see what it was all about.

"Señors ... Señoras ... Señoritas ... Señoritos," the Bull-grower shouted, "I am so jollico to announcio that Lunes Martes Miercoles Jueves Sabado Domingo Barcelo, son of Don Navidad Lunes Barcelo the Famous Matador, will challenge El Sarten the Terrrrrrrrrrrrrrrrrrrífico Bullico in the arenico."

Having made the announcement, Señor Martillo galloped away to the next town to say it all over again.

The people of El Zapato didn't laugh as loudly as one might have expected when they heard the news. Instead, they wondered if Zonta would land up in a Naranja tree west of El Zapato or north of El Zapato.

"The Little Matador is lighter, therefore he will travel farther," they argued, and gambled accordingly.

When Señorita Estrella heard the news she was at first alarmed, then she became very proud of Zonta, then she wrote her first letter.

"Dear Little Matador.
You are the bravest person I know.
I love you very much. Oh, very, very much.
Your Estrella."

This, of course, made Zonta feel twice as brave and ten times more daring. Every day he practised and practised, determined to bring honour and fame to the name of Barcelo once again. At first he practised with baby bulls, then medium-sized bulls, and then large, fat, fierce bulls. When Don Barcelo saw how skilful his son was becoming in the art of matadoring, he shouted encouragement from the top of the Castillo.

"Bravo . . . bravo, my Zonta . . .!"

Then he shaved off his long beard. Once more he grew smooth black side-whiskers that curled towards his aristocratic nose.

Zonta's beautiful mother, who had always something clever on the end of her tongue, whispered:

"Practise makes perfect, my son."

So Zonta practised and became perfect. His parents became very happy and used the same spiral staircase again. This made Zonta very happy, but the happiest moment of his life was still to come.

Twenty–second Capitulo

In one night Zonta, the Little Matador, became as famous as Sarten the Terrrrrifico Bull.

And in one night Señorita Estrella really believed that one day she would marry the brave Zonta. She sent him a special letter on her best note-paper. The letter was delivered by a Turtle Dove who lived in an Orange Tree.

"The Little White House
Surrounded by Naranja Trees
El Zapato. Spain.

Dear Little Matador,
　　　　Every morning at six o'clock, and every evening at six o'clock, I will go to Father Potelo's church and pray for you.

Your Estrella."

And so, one evening, Zonta followed Estrella to church, and they met face to face for the first time in their lives. For each one there was a great surprise.

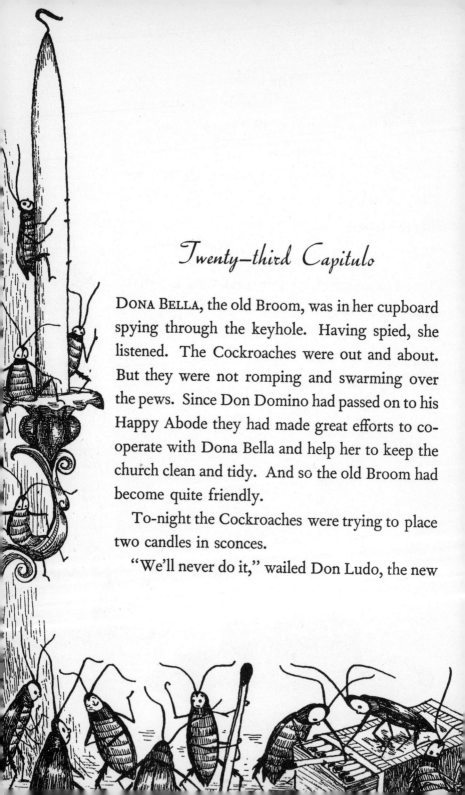

Twenty–third Capitulo

DONA BELLA, the old Broom, was in her cupboard spying through the keyhole. Having spied, she listened. The Cockroaches were out and about. But they were not romping and swarming over the pews. Since Don Domino had passed on to his Happy Abode they had made great efforts to co-operate with Dona Bella and help her to keep the church clean and tidy. And so the old Broom had become quite friendly.

To-night the Cockroaches were trying to place two candles in sconces.

"We'll never do it," wailed Don Ludo, the new

Leader. "We may as well try and put sixpence on the moon."

But a Cockroach called Juan had climbed to an oak beam above the altar. Sitting astride his perch, he lowered a piece of string to the floor.

"Tie the candles on the end, Don Ludo," he called. "Then help me hoist them to the sconces. This is how the Egyptians built the Pyramids."

"What a clever fellow you are!" cried Don Ludo. "Why didn't we think of this in the first place? All together—pull."

With this simple device, the candles were swung to the sconces.

"What on earth are they playing at?" said Dona Bella to herself in her cupboard.

Quietly, she lifted the cupboard latch and peered out. She listened. Don Ludo was speaking.

"That's all very well; the candles are in the sconces, but who's going to be brave enough to light them? That's a tricky business. Matches explode in a blinding flash. Very dangerous. I've seen Father Potelo burn his fingers."

There was a long silence. Don Ludo looked from one to the other.

"Any volunteers?" he asked.

The Cockroaches shook their heads. Then they looked up at the unlit candles and shook their heads again.

"May I be of any assistance?"

The sudden appearance of Dona Bella sent the Cockroaches fleeing in panic to the pulpit.

"*Dios mio* . . . The Broom . . . Run. . . ."

But in a kind voice, Dona Bella called them back.

"Don't be afraid. I'd like to help. Allow ME to light the candles."

Don Ludo peered round a pillar.

"W-w-would you r-r-really?" he asked.

"Certainly."

And taking up the matches Dona Bella struck a light.

"For whom is the first candle?"

"It is for the Little Matador and Sarten the Bull," cried the Cockroaches from the pulpit.

"And the second one?" asked the Broom.

"That is for you, you being our enemy. We must teach ourselves to love our enemies."

At this Dona Bella burst into tears.

"Thank . . . you," she stammered, and taking a third candle she lit it and placed it in a sconce beside the others.

"That's for all of you from me."

With that she rushed off to her cupboard and wept until she was the happiest broom in all El Zapato.

Don Ludo gasped.

"I really believe she likes us, after all. What a beautiful old Broom she is."

One by one the Cockroaches stole out from the pulpit to gaze up at THEIR candle. The large yellow flame burned brightly and shed its light upon the Cockroaches gathered before the altar.

"Don Domino was quite right," said Don Ludo. "If you want peace try and love your enemies."

As he finished speaking, the Town Hall clock began

to strike . . . ONE . . . TWO . . . THREE . . .
FOUR . . .

On the stroke of six the church doors opened.
"*Cuidado . . . cuidado!*" cried Juan.

The vast army of Cockroaches scattered in all directions as down the aisle came the sound of footsteps.

Juan looked out round a leg of a pew.

"It's the Little Matador and Señorita Estrella," he whispered to Don Ludo. "They do look surprised to see one another."

And this was perfectly true. They had never stood so close together before. How beautiful she was and how handsome the Little Matador. Zonta opened his mouth as if to speak her name. Oh, how he tried to say "Estrella!" But all he could do was to shake his head in dismay. Turning to a dusty pew, he wrote with his finger:

"I can't talk, Estrella."

When she read these words, Estrella looked up at Zonta. Smiling, she shook her head. Then, in the same dust, she wrote:

"Neither can I."

And they both shook their heads and smiled.

Taking Estrella by the hand, Zonta led her to the
altar to pray.

The Cockroaches smiled.

"They're in love," said Don Ludo.

The Cockroaches nodded.

Twenty—fourth Capitulo

TO THE BULLFIGHT . . . . . TO THE BULLFIGHT . . . TO THE BULLFIGHT.

TO-DAY

LA CORRIDA DE TOROS

PERSONAL APPEARANCE

of

ZONTA

The Little Matador

and

EL SARTEN

The Terrrrrrrifico Bull

On every Naranja tree, and on every spare wall along the winding road to Madrid, Señor Martillo pasted posters with paste made from plain flour. From tree to tree and from wall to wall he galloped on his fine Black Caballo, the one that was born in Portugal. On the right side of the saddle there was a bucket of paste, on the left side of the saddle there was a long paste-brush. Round Señor Martillo's neck there hung a large satchel with posters in it.

"For goodness' sake be careful!" cried the fine Black Caballo in Portuguese. "You're splashing me from head to hooves with that sticky paste."

"Terrrrrrribly sorry," shouted Señor Martillo, who was very jolly to-day. "I've got a terrrribly careless brush. Ho, ho! Ho, ho, ho! Ha, ha, ha, ha! . . . I'm so happico, my beautiful Caballico."

"And I'm so stickio."

"Terrrrribly sorry."

So on they went from tree to tree until they reached Madrid.

That same morning, when the dawn peeped over the horizon, a grand procession of people, carts, donkeys, mules and horses left El Zapato for the Bullring at Madrid. There were guitar-players, singers, dancers, flute-players and police-men, all in their holiday attire. Leading the procession on magnificent Caballos that were gaily caparisoned, was the famous family of Barcelos. Close behind, on white mules, came Father Potelo,

Señorita Estrella, the Schoolmaster and Doctor Bomba. The Doctor carried a large pair of binoculars round his neck just in case something odd happened. Looking very handsome and brave in the uniform of a Matador, Zonta acknowledged the cheering crowds from his prancing Caballo.

"*Vaya Vd con Dios!*"

"May all go well with you!"

Dona Barcelo whispered in her son's ear:

"He who looks before he leaps knows where he is going to land. An old Spanish proverb, my Zonta. There is also another one, one your grandmother often quoted. Don't give a foot when a toe will do."

Then Don Barcelo whispered in his son's ear:

"If you are tossed out of the Bullring try and land on your feet and not your head. It is better."

Zonta nodded, then he gazed upon Estrella and smiled.

*

The sun shone on the yellow sand in the arena. The fine ladies of Spain sat in the Grandstands, their beautifully embroidered shawls spread out before them on the balustrades. The gallant gentlemen and Caballeros of Spain also sat in the Grandstands beside their ladies. The poor people sat on stone seats and cheered. Señorita Estrella sat on a cushion beside her Papa and Father Potelo. She wore a mantilla on her hair and a rose behind her ear—the one on the left. El Sarten waited in his stable, more determined than ever that Zonta should receive the Little Cockroach's message.

Outside in the arena, Señor Martillo blew his long trumpet. The bullfight was about to begin.

Dressed in magnificent clothes that were embroidered in gold, red and blue, a black hat on his head and a red cape lying on his left shoulder, came Zonta, the Little Matador. He was escorted by two tall, thin Matadors of some renown. They had hooked noses and brave hearts. Following came the Banderilleros, as resplendent as the Matadors in their own particular dress. The courageous Picadors, each armed with a long lance, rode on old Caballos. They looked like Don Quixotes or Knights of Old. Last of all marched the attendants. They wore blue trousers, vermilion shirts, and red hats with blue knobs. They led spare horses with bright-coloured saddles. As the procession moved across the arena the crowds cheered the Little Matador:

"Bravo, Zonta!... May it go well with you....
Bravo!"

The ladies threw flowers into the arena. Estrella threw a rose, the one from behind her left ear. Zonta picked it up, sighed, and put it in his pocket for luck. Don Barcelo and his beautiful wife waved. The crowds cheered and cheered and cheered.

The Proud Bull-grower blew his long trumpet.

"Ta tatata ta. Rah tra riddle ee omp."

Immediately the stables were thrown open and the enormous, terrifying Sarten romped into the Bullring, bellowing with all his might. The Matadors, the Banderilleros and the Picadors trembled. Zonta's large eyes went round and round like wild windmills.

"Look out!" roared the crowd.

Seeing the Little Matador, Sarten kicked up his heels and charged across the arena. But long before he reached Zonta, a Picador galloped out

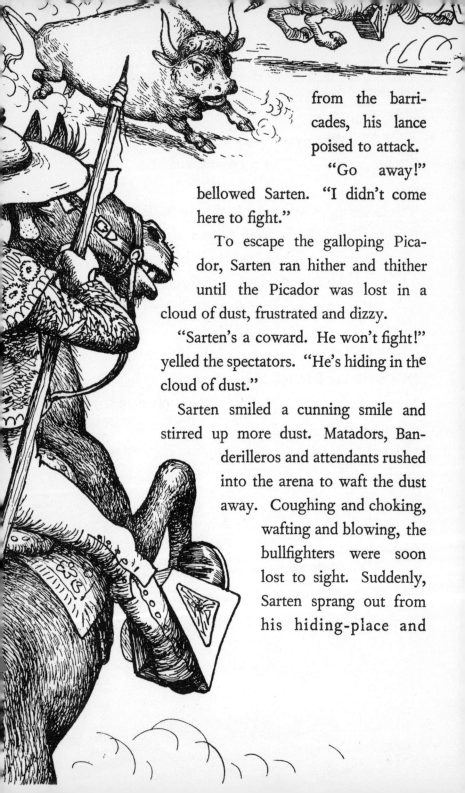

from the barricades, his lance poised to attack.

"Go away!" bellowed Sarten. "I didn't come here to fight."

To escape the galloping Picador, Sarten ran hither and thither until the Picador was lost in a cloud of dust, frustrated and dizzy.

"Sarten's a coward. He won't fight!" yelled the spectators. "He's hiding in the cloud of dust."

Sarten smiled a cunning smile and stirred up more dust. Matadors, Banderilleros and attendants rushed into the arena to waft the dust away. Coughing and choking, wafting and blowing, the bullfighters were soon lost to sight. Suddenly, Sarten sprang out from his hiding-place and charged towards the Little Matador. Standing alone, Zonta faced the terrifying bull. With skill and grace he swung round on his toes to make a beautiful pass as Sarten charged harmlessly by.

"Bravo! . . . bravo! . . .

"Ole! . . . ole! . . . ole!"

"Well done! . . . Bravo!"

The excitement grew as the Little Matador made more beautiful passes with his vermilion cape. As swift as a hare, as smooth as an eel, Zonta played the bull with renewed skill. The crowds roared their delight.

"Bravo!"

Bewildered and fuzzled, Sarten paused to seek out the Little Matador. Then a Galloping Picador galloped out from a dust-cloud and jabbed the unsuspecting bull with his lance.

"OUCH!!"

At the same time, Sarten saw the Little Matador at

the far end of the arena. Spurred on by the Picador, Sarten put all his speed into his four legs and careered towards Zonta.

"I have a message," he bellowed. "I have a message."

The next moment came quickly. Whoosh! Sarten thundered past the vermilion cape into the stout wooden barricades. Stunned, the great bull went down like a log. Up went the spectators' hats.

"*Magnifico*. . . . Ole! . . . Bravo!"

Slowly, more fuzzled and bewildered than ever, Sarten staggered to his feet. A thousand stars danced before him. His eyes watered. His head ached. He felt dizzy.

"Oh dear. Where am I?"

He shook his great, big head. The stars vanished. His eyes cleared. There, immediately in front of him, a shining sword in his hand, stood the brave Little Matador. Sarten paused, a look of fear in his eyes.

"Don't kill me," he pleaded. "I didn't

come here to fight. I've got a message for you from a Little Cockroach."

The sword wavered in Zonta's hand as he gaped open-mouthed. Excitement grew around the vast arena. The fine gentlemen and fine ladies of Spain waited breathlessly for the Little Matador to kill the bull. Sarten moved slowly towards Zonta.

"Don't kill me," he pleaded again. "Don't kill me."

Then came a great gasp of horror from the crowds. The shining sword fell from Zonta's hand. Unarmed, and unafraid, he faced the Terrrifico Bull. Don Barcelo sprang to his feet.

"The sword, my son. The sword!"

The Matadors, the Banderilleros and the Picadors peered over the barricades, unable to believe their eyes. Zonta awaited the approaching Sarten.

"*Cuidado! ... Cuidado!*" they shouted. "LOOK OUT! Pick up the sword!"

As Sarten stepped on to the point of the sword as it lay on the yellow sand, he halted abruptly. A thousand frowns knitted his massive brow.

"Ooooh! ... Oh! ... I've forgotten the message. I've forgotten the Little Cockroach's message," he cried, and he shook his head, and he tossed his head in dismay.

The message he had recited so carefully to himself for a whole week was lost on his tongue. Mortified with grief, he broke down and wept bitterly.

"OOOOOOOh! . . . OOOOOOOh!" he sobbed, "OOOOOh! . . . OOOOOh!"

"What is going on out there?" asked the fine Black Caballo in Portuguese.

But Señor Martillo was too astonished to answer. Zonta was kneeling before the Terrrifico Bull.

"You must remember. Think of the Little Cockroach. . . . Think . . . think. . . ."

Then, as if he had suddenly been scared out of himself, Zonta sprang to his feet, a look of great amazement on his face.

"I spoke. . . . I spoke!" he shouted. "My tongue spoke!!!!!"

Excitedly he turned to Sarten.

"I did speak, didn't I?"

"Yes, yes, you did," sobbed Sarten, still trying to remember the Cockroach's message.

"I can talk!" cried Zonta, and he clapped his hands and danced round the Terrrrifico Bull.

Don Barcelo blinked unbelievingly. The astonished crowds blinked, rubbed their eyes, then blinked again. Doctor Bomba gaped through his large binoculars and said, "Odder than odd." Zonta raced across the arena.

"Papa . . . Mama . . . Estrella!"

Don Barcelo's wide sombrero flew off his head in amazement.

"Did you say 'Papa'?"

"Yes, Papa. I can talk."

And the beautiful Dona Barcelo said:

"Did you say 'Mama'?"

"Yes, Mama."

Don Barcelo smiled a smile as wide as a large piece of melon.

"He said 'Mama'. I heard him."

But Señorita Estrella sobbed:

"Oh, Zonta. I wish I could talk, too. If only. . . ."

Zonta smiled. He took her hand and whispered:

"You can."

"Can I really? ... Oh, dear ... I spoke!"

"It's a miracle," cried Father Potelo, and he lifted Estrella up into his arms. "A MIRACLE has happened!" he roared into the Schoolmaster's ear. "Estrella can SPEAK."

Astounded, the spectators gaped, gasped, blinked and stared from one to the other.

Then came a terrifying bellow. Sarten threw his hind legs in the air, he skipped and jumped, bellowed and gambolled.

"I've remembered!" he shouted and raced up to Zonta.

"The Little Cockroach said, '*We must learn to love our enemies and to tread carefully, lest we tread on a friend!*'"

And with his head held high, his eyes shining happily, Sarten the Terrrrrifico Bull danced merrily away to the stables.

"Hey!" shouted the fine Black Caballo. "Where do you think you're going? You haven't been killed yet."

"I'm excused," said Sarten. "Good afternoon!"

"Well, I'll blow a trumpet!" said the Caballo from Portugal. "I'll bet he gets a pension, too."

And so ended the most remarkable Bullfight. The message from Don Domino made the people think—even Señor Martillo began to think. On the way home to the Campo, the Bull-grower and the fine Black Caballo travelled in Sarten's cage. When they passed El Zapato they were singing together.

"Oh, I will grow Naranjas, Naranjas, Naranjas,
   I will grow Naranjas,
And give them to my loves.
Oh, oh, Naranjas, sweet, sweet Naranjas,
   I will grow Naranjas,
And give them all away."

And following came the happiest people in Spain: Don Barcelo and his beautiful wife, the Schoolmaster, Father Potelo, and Señorita Estrella and Zonta, the Little Matador.

Twenty-fifth Capitulo

FOUR years later, when all the Naranja trees were in blossom, Estrella married Zonta in Father Potelo's Little White Church. Dona Bella, the Broom, saw the ceremony through the keyhole in her cupboard. The Cockroaches waited outside and cheered. The Campana in the belfry went

Ding dong ding! dong ding dong! when Estrella and Zonta rode away on their beautiful prancing Caballos that were gaily caparisoned.

"Clippety clop ... clippety clop."

From the top of the Old Castillo, Don Barcelo and his wife waved as the two young lovers galloped away across the Campo to be very, very happy.

THE END

Boas Noites. Good night (Portuguese).

Buenas noches. Good night.

Caballero. Horseman.

Caballo. Horse.

Campana. Bell.

Campo. Country.

Capitulo. Chapter.

Caramba! Heavens!

Castillo. Castle.

Cuidado. Be careful.

Dios mio. Good gracious!

Domingo. Sunday.

Esto com pressa. I am in a hurry (Portuguese).

Hasta mañana. Until to-morrow.

Jueves, Viernes, Sabado. Thursday, Friday, Saturday.

La Corrida de Toros. The Bullfight.

Lunes, Martes, Miercoles. Monday, Tuesday, Wednesday.

Naranja. Orange.

Navidad. Christmas.

Primavera. Spring.

Verano. Summer.

Boas Noites.   Good night (Portuguese).

Buenas noches.   Good night.

Caballero.   Horseman.

Caballo.   Horse.

Campana.   Bell.

Campo.   Country.

Capitulo.   Chapter.

Caramba!   Heavens!

Castillo.   Castle.

Cuidado.   Be careful.

Dios mio.   Good gracious!

Domingo.   Sunday.

Esto com pressa.   I am in a hurry (Portuguese).

Hasta mañana.   Until to-morrow.

Jueves, Viernes, Sabado.   Thursday, Friday, Saturday.

La Corrida de Toros.   The Bullfight.

Lunes, Martes, Miercoles.   Monday, Tuesday, Wednesday.

Naranja.   Orange.

Navidad.   Christmas.

Primavera.   Spring.

Verano.   Summer.